Disney

FROZEN

Adventures on Ice

Stories and Activities from Arendelle and Beyond!

we make books come alive®
Phoenix International Publications, Inc.
Chicago • London • New York • Hamburg • Mexico City • Sydney

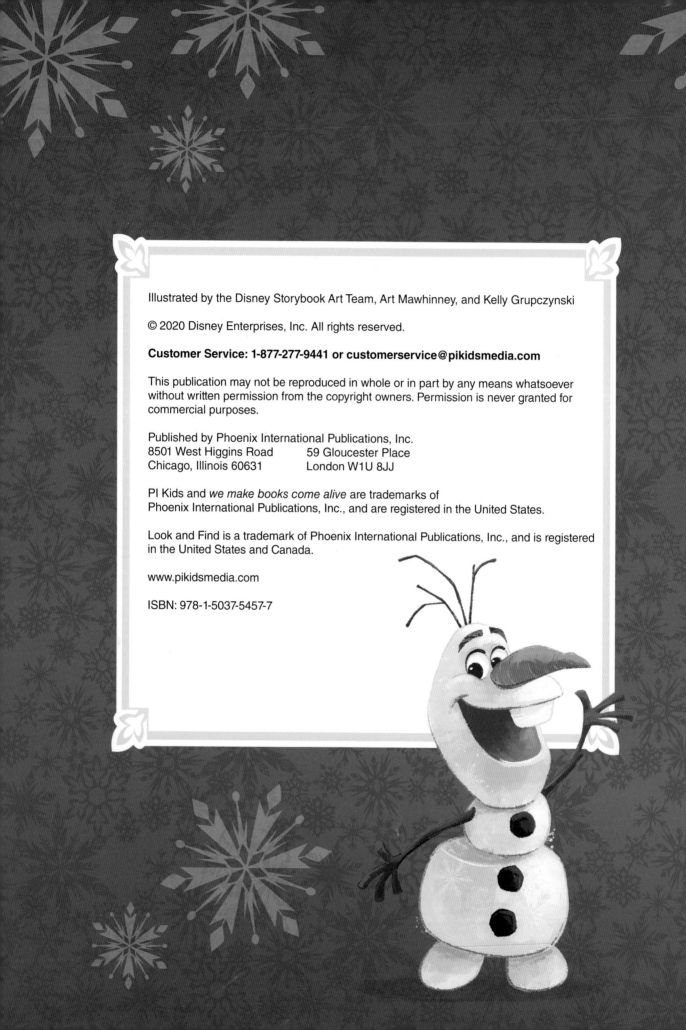

Illustrated by the Disney Storybook Art Team, Art Mawhinney, and Kelly Grupczynski

Customer Service: 1-877-277-9441 or customerservice@pikidsmedia.com

Published by Phoenix International Publications, Inc.
8501 West Higgins Road   59 Gloucester Place
Chicago, Illinois 60631   London W1U 8JJ

PI Kids and *we make books come alive* are trademarks of
Phoenix International Publications, Inc., and are registered in the United States.

Look and Find is a trademark of Phoenix International Publications, Inc., and is registered in the United States and Canada.

www.pikidsmedia.com

ISBN: 978-1-5037-5457-7

Table of Contents

Frozen

$\mathcal{T}$he king and queen of Arendelle are keeping a secret. Their elder daughter Elsa has a magical power she can't always control. She can make ice and snow!

After an accident, Elsa wants to protect her little sister Anna from her magic. So she stops playing with Anna, and the two sisters grow apart.

Years later, on the day Elsa is crowned Queen of Arendelle, Anna meets Prince Hans. She falls in love, and they decide to marry.

When Anna tells Elsa the news, the sisters argue. Elsa's magic breaks loose, freezing the kingdom!

Quickly, Elsa flees into the mountains, where she makes a new realm of ice and snow for herself.

Anna follows her sister to try to bring her home.

On Anna's journey, she meets Kristoff, his reindeer Sven, and Olaf, a talking snowman. Together, they find Elsa's ice palace… and Elsa.

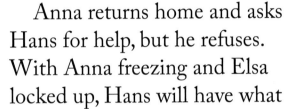

Anna begs Elsa to come home, but Elsa refuses. As she sends Anna away, Elsa accidentally hits her with an icy blast.

After Anna leaves, Hans appears— and captures Elsa!

Now both sisters are in trouble. Elsa's blast is turning Anna into ice! The only thing that can save her is an act of true love.

Anna returns home and asks Hans for help, but he refuses. With Anna freezing and Elsa locked up, Hans will have what he wants most: the crown of Arendelle.

Anna searches for Kristoff, but instead she finds Elsa, who has escaped.

As Hans raises his sword over Elsa, Anna blocks the blow—just as her body freezes completely. Hans's blade shatters! Anna is saved, and the kingdom is, too!

Anna's own act of love for her sister has melted the icy spell forever.

AN ACT OF TRUE LOVE CAN THAW A FROZEN HEART.

People from all over the world have come to Arendelle for Elsa's coronation. Find Prince Hans and these other visitors and supplies:

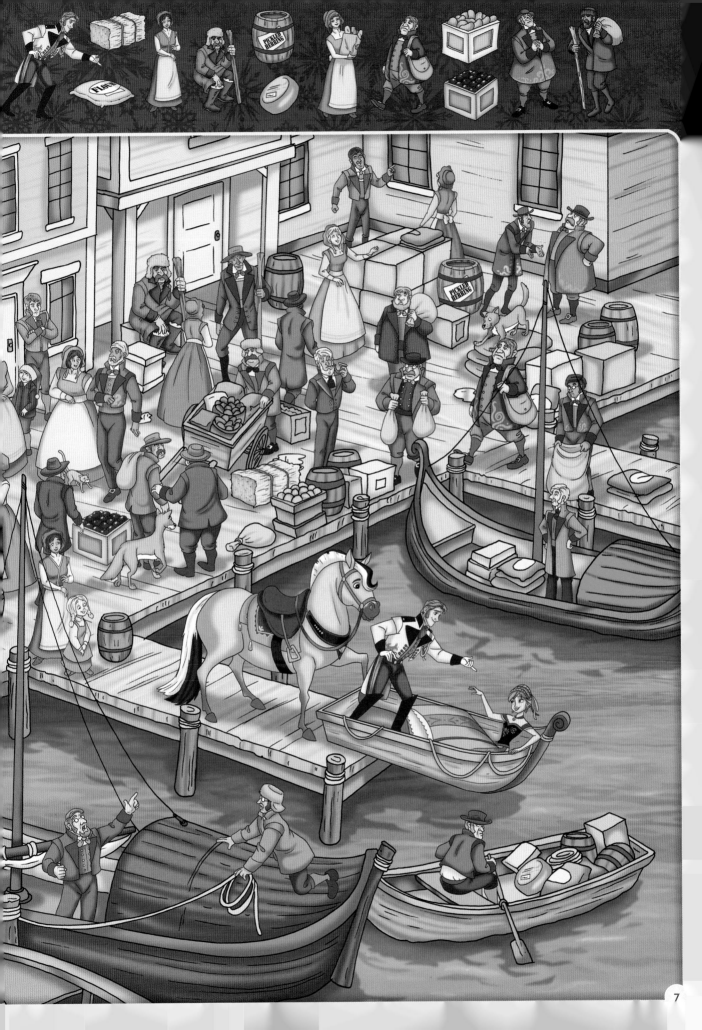

Anna and Kristoff go to look for Anna after Elsa flees Arendelle... but the wolves find them first! While they make their escape, look for Kristoff's scattered belongings amongst these animal tracks:

8

The sisters are together again, and summer has returned to Arendelle! To thank Kristoff for helping her, Anna gives him a brand-new sled. Look around town for these other gifts, and for these loving sister pairs:

Anna and Elsa

Snow Angels

Little Princesses Elsa and Anna are supposed to be playing quietly in their rooms while their parents entertain important visitors. But they're slipping and sliding, and having fun with Elsa's magic instead!

First, Elsa adds a row of ice statues to the castle art gallery. The ice sculptures surprise and impress the visiting Baron of Snoob.

"Reee-markable!" he says.

His wife, Baroness Bertilda, just sniffs. Very loudly. Next, Elsa and Anna scamper into the kitchen.

"Let's have a snowball fight!" says Anna. Elsa fills the room with huge snowdrifts. When the tour party reaches the kitchen, the girls are gone, but the snowballs are still there.

"Deee-licious!" exclaims the baron. "Thank you for giving us an icy treat on a warm summer's day!"

The baroness sniffs again…but she still eats her snow cup.

Now the girls run into the ballroom. Soon they are climbing up Elsa's ice hills, and sliding down again.

"Let's make snow angels!" says Anna.

As the royal visitors enter the ballroom, Baroness Bertilda slips on the snow.

The King and Queen rush to her side. But before they can apologize…

"Snow angels!" Bertilda cries. "I love snow angels! Let's make some more!"

"Deee-lightful!" chuckles the baron. "Arendelle certainly knows how to make its visitors feel at home!"

That night, the King looks at his sleeping daughters and whispers, "Who would have thought a palace filled with snow could be a good thing?"

"Leave it to our little snow angels!" the Queen says with a smile.

DO YOU WANT TO BUILD A SNOWMAN?

Look around for some things that Anna would like to share with her sister, and some things she enjoys doing solo:

PICTURE PUZZLE

Look for 10 differences between these wintry scenes.

PICTURE PUZZLE

Search these cozy pictures to find 10 differences.

Answer key: comb, book under table, yarn, popcorn piece, saucer, slippers, hairbrush, bookmark, design on bookshelf, carpet pattern

Olaf

Olaf's Dream

Most snowmen are found only in wintertime. After all, if you're made of snow and you want to stay that way, an icy winter breeze is your best friend!

But Olaf is a different kind of snowman. Olaf dreams about summer.

He loves to imagine feeling summer's sun on his face… making sand angels…and chasing warm waves at the beach.

One wintry day, Olaf meets Anna. And on that day, his summer dreams begin to come true.

Anna's sister Elsa fled into the mountains after accidentally freezing the kingdom. Olaf helps the sisters find each other again.

Then Anna is betrayed by Prince Hans. Olaf builds a big fire to keep her from freezing.

"Some people are worth melting for," he says.

After summer returns to Arendelle, Queen Elsa isn't about to let a good friend like Olaf melt away.

With a magical wave of her hands, Elsa gives Olaf his very own snow flurry. It follows him wherever he goes, all year long!

Now Olaf can enjoy autumn, winter, spring—and summer too. Summer is even better than Olaf dreamed it could be, now that he can share it with his friends!

I'VE ALWAYS LOVED THE IDEA OF SUMMER!

PICTURE PUZZLE

Can you see 10 differences between these sandy scenes?

It might seem a little strange for a snowman to like sunny weather, but Elsa gives Olaf his own personal snow flurry, and now he's *always* cool! Dig up these castle-building tools and spy these sunshine-loving sidekicks:

Olaf is posing for a new portrait—painted by Anna! Soon his picture will be on display in Arendelle's Gallery of Friends. Can you find these works, and the supplies used to make them?

Land and Sea Adventures

A Royal Visit

For months, Elsa and Anna have been planning a royal visit to three neighboring kingdoms. Now it's time to go!

The sisters' first stop is Zaria, with a warm seaside welcome from King Stebor and Queen Renalia.

Zaria is known for its ever-blooming gardens. At a party that evening, flowers fill the royal ballroom with color and perfume.

"Lilies, roses, and bright blue bellflowers!" says Elsa at dinner. "I've never seen such beautiful flowers at this time of year!"

"Not even in Arendelle?" asks Queen Renalia.

"Arendelle is too snowy for year-round flowers," says Anna.

Next, the sisters sail to Chatho, where Queen Colisa takes them on a tour.

"Our parks are filled with wild creatures," Colisa tells Anna and Elsa. "Here you see Chatho's national animal, *Slothus serendipitous*. Do you have sloths in Arendelle?"

"Ummm…Arendelle isn't warm enough for sloths," says Anna. "But we have lots of reindeer!"

At Vakretta, their last stop, Anna and Elsa are treated to the city's famous lemonade. Elsa adds a special touch to each glass: magical ice!

"Do you drink lemonade in Arendelle?" asks the mayor.

"We're more of a hot chocolate kind of kingdom," says Anna.

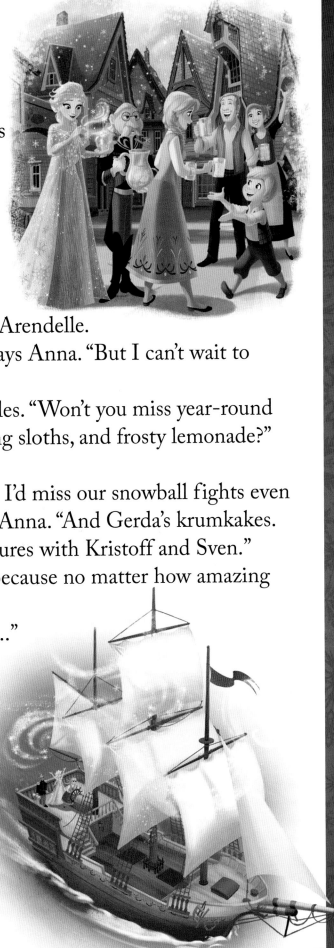

Soon the sisters are sailing back to Arendelle.

"What lovely neighbors we have!" says Anna. "But I can't wait to get home."

Elsa smiles. "Won't you miss year-round roses, smiling sloths, and frosty lemonade?" she asks.

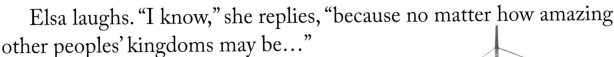

"Yes, but I'd miss our snowball fights even more," says Anna. "And Gerda's krumkakes. And adventures with Kristoff and Sven."

Elsa laughs. "I know," she replies, "because no matter how amazing other peoples' kingdoms may be…"

"…and they can be awfully amazing…" Anna says.

"…there's no place like home!" the sisters say together.

"With or without sloths!" Anna adds.

THERE'S NO PLACE LIKE HOME!

Life in Arendelle is full of fun! Look around for Elsa and Anna, and their playful pals:

Anna and Elsa are sailing across the fjord, with Olaf at the helm! Can you spot these colorful waterside residents and these helpful way-finding tools?

PICTURE PUZZLE

Answer key: sun, flag, birds, tower, boat design, Elsa's cape, fish, gull's wing, anchor, Olaf's arm

All Are Invited!

Sister Surprise

One wintry evening, Anna and Elsa sit together by the fire.

I would love to give Elsa a great big surprise, thinks Anna.

It's time I did something really special for Anna, thinks Elsa.

Anna has a great idea. She'll throw a surprise party for Elsa! All of their friends will come.

Anna bakes Elsa's favorite sweets. Olaf helps by taking the cookies out of the oven when they're done.

Elsa also has a great idea. She'll throw a surprise party for Anna! The best musicians will play. Elsa decides to make a special ice sculpture. Kristoff helps her with the ice.

It's party time! The guests gather in the castle ballroom. When Anna and Elsa walk in, everyone yells "Surprise!"— including Anna and Elsa.

"I planned this party for you," says Anna.

"And I planned it for you!" says Elsa.
The sisters laugh and eat and dance with all of their friends.

"We both had the same great idea," says Elsa.

"But I missed you while we were busy party planning," says Anna. "Let's make sure to plan our next surprise together!"

SHE'S MY
SISTER!

Elsa's favorite thing about royal parties is decorating! Find these ice sculptures and pretty snowflakes she's making for the Winter Ball:

The Winter Ball is fun for everyone! Search the party for these delightful designs and these pairs of dancers:

Cookies are here, there, and everywhere! Can you spot these cookie-making supplies and these toothsome tidbits?

Trolls

Troll Troubles

"You're babysitting the trolls?" Elsa asks her sister Anna. "That sounds like a big job to me." But Anna isn't worried. She and Kristoff are watching the troll babies while their parents go to a magical meeting. How hard can that be?

In Troll Valley, Bulda thinks it will be a quiet night. "The babies should be asleep soon," she tells Anna and Kristoff.

Anna waves as the grown-up trolls say goodbye.

"Don't worry about us!" Anna says. "I'm sure we won't have any problems."

"Uh, Anna?" says Kristoff. "We have nothing *but* problems. Look!"

Anna turns around. The troll babies have escaped from their playpen. They're climbing and crawling *everywhere!*

"Hurry!" says Anna. "We need to round them up."

But the more Anna, Kristoff, and Sven try to calm down the troll tots, the wilder they become!

"Maybe they're hungry," Anna suggests.

"Maybe they need a leaf change," Kristoff guesses.

"Maybe they're tired," says Anna. "Let's put them to bed."

Suddenly the frazzled friends hear a familiar voice. It's Olaf!

"Hey, can I help?" Olaf calls.

"Yes, please!" says Anna. "Do you know any bedtime stories?"

Olaf tells the tots a story about summer. "Imagine rocking in a hammock on a sunny beach," he says. "Back and forth… back and forth…"

Soon the tots are blinking sleepy eyes.

KEEP YOUR COOL!

"Quick, Kristoff!" Anna whispers. "Sing them a lullaby."

Kristoff picks up his lute and starts to play.

By the time the grown-up trolls return, everything is peaceful.

"You were right, Bulda," says Anna. "We had a quiet night with the tots…"

"…once they finally fell asleep!" says Kristoff with a big grin.

Anna and Kristoff like to visit Kristoff's family in Troll Valley. While everyone says hello, look for these trolls amongst these magically shaped rocks:

What a special night to enjoy the Northern Lights and some campfire songs with the trolls. Twinkle, twinkle, little fireflies! See if you can find these six tiny sparklers, and these human-made lights, too:

Winter Wonder

A Starry Night

Anna, Elsa, and Olaf are so excited. It's almost time to see the Northern Lights glowing in the sky! The friends hurry from the castle to ride with Kristoff and Sven to Troll Valley.

"The Northern Lights are best seen on clear nights," Kristoff says to Anna, Elsa, and Olaf. "And Troll Valley is the best place to see them."

"Great!" says Anna. "But first, let's get a lantern, so we can see where we're going."

Sven stops at Oaken's Trading Post so the friends can buy a lantern.

"Surprise, Kristoff!" Anna and Elsa exclaim. "We also had your lute tuned so you can play for us tonight."

"Hoo-hoo! You better hurry," Oaken says, "so you will see all the pretty lights, and have good feelings!"

When the friends finally arrive in Troll Valley, the sun has set, the moon is high, and the Northern Lights are up in the sky! The troll tots are so excited.

"The sky is awake, the sky is awake, what a pretty sight it makes!" all the trolls chant.

As the lights glow, the sisters each look for a star and make a wish. Then they dance with Olaf while Kristoff plays.

"What did you wish for, Olaf?" Anna asks.

"Nothing," says Olaf. "I have everything I could wish for, because my friends are right here with me!"

THE SKY'S AWAKE!

Sven loves being a part of Kristoff's adventures.

Olaf can't wait to find friendship, sunshine, and warm hugs. In the meantime, can you spot these animal onlookers among these chilly crystals?

When Princess Anna first discovers her sister Elsa's magical power, she thinks it's wonderful! Look around to find these icy playthings and these snowman-building items:

Fun with Friends

Olaf's New Friend

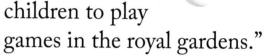

"Hi Anna! Hi Elsa!" Olaf calls to his friends. "Do you want to pick flowers with me up in the mountains? The crocuses are blooming! Don't you just love springtime?"

"I'd love to pick flowers with you, Olaf," says Elsa. "But I've invited the village children to play games in the royal gardens."

"I'm sorry, but I can't go flower picking with you either," says Anna. "Kristoff and I promised to babysit the little trolls."

"That's OK. I'll find someone to pick flowers with," says Olaf, as a bumblebee buzzes by. "Hey, I bet that bee knows where the best flowers are."

Olaf follows the bee way up the mountain and—whoops!

Just as Olaf starts tumbling down the mountain, a little reindeer comes along. Quickly, the reindeer gathers up a bunch of crocuses to give Olaf a nice soft place to land.

"Thanks!" says Olaf to the reindeer. "Hey, do you want to meet my friends?" Together, they climb down the mountain.

"Hi Anna! Hi Elsa!" Olaf calls. "Come meet my new friend. He saved me from a tumble. And even better…he likes picking flowers!"

I LIKE WARM HUGS!!

PICTURE PUZZLE

Anna, Elsa, and Olaf have made some new friends: a family of ducks!

Can you spot 10 differences between these springtime scenes?

Today Arendelle is celebrating Winter in Summer Day, with treats just as chilly as Olaf. Do you see these delicious desserts and these yummy fresh fruits?

Winter in Summer Day!

Everybody wants to win the bubble-blowing contest. Just be careful you don't end up IN a bubble! Can you find these airborne articles, inside and outside the bubbles?

Which *Frozen* Character Are YOU?

Are you most like:

Anna

Anna is a **loyal**, **determined**, and **daring** free spirit. She will never give up on a friend or a sister, and she always finds the strength to do the next right thing when faced with the impossible. Anna is known for her can-do attitude, and she has learned that an act of true love can thaw a frozen heart.

Elsa

Elsa works hard to be a good ruler, sister, and friend. Although she can seem **quiet**, she has swirling emotions deep inside that you'll discover when you get to know her, and she is **strong** and **fierce** when she sets her snowy power free. With a heart that is bigger than she knows, Elsa follows her destiny into the unknown.

Olaf

This snowman loves warm hugs! Elsa created him with her magic, and he has been a true friend ever since. Funny, curious, and full of wonder, Olaf has a kind word for everyone he meets. He is full of questions, and even fears, but he never lets them come between him and the people he loves.

Kristoff

Before he meets Anna, Kristoff doesn't know many people—in fact, he tends to prefer reindeer. But once he and Anna become friends, Kristoff proves himself to be caring, honest, and brave. He doesn't always know the right thing to say, but he is ready to spring into action when you need him.

Sven

Sven always knows just what Kristoff is thinking. And with a simple snort or tilt of his antlers, Sven is able to communicate what's on his mind. This friendly, lovable, and opinionated reindeer is always ready to share the adventure... and the carrots.

King Agnarr tells young Elsa and Anna a story from a long time ago. When he was a boy, King Agnarr's father built a dam to help the forest-dwelling Northuldra people. After the dam was completed, there was a battle between the Northuldra and the Arendellians, and the forest became covered in mist, locked from the outside world. But why? Elsa wonders about the forest.

One day, Elsa hears a voice calling to her. As she reaches out to it with her powers, a shockwave suddenly blasts through Arendelle! The wind blows against the kingdom, its fire and water are taken, and the earth ripples its streets.

Hoping to save Arendelle, Elsa and Anna set off for the forest with Olaf, Kristoff, and Sven.

"Promise me we'll do this together," Anna says.

"I promise," says Elsa.

At the edge of the Enchanted Forest, a wall of mist opens before Anna and Elsa. But once the friends pass through, the mist closes again, trapping them in the woods!

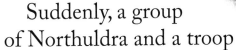

Suddenly, a group of Northuldra and a troop of Arendellian soldiers take them by surprise. Both sides have been stuck in the forest since the battle King Agnarr told of. And each side blames the other!

The sisters hope to free everyone trapped in the forest by finding the voice that calls to Elsa. They travel north with Olaf while Kristoff and Sven stay in the forest.

Soon, Elsa and Anna find their parents' shipwreck! They learn that their parents were searching for the mystical river Ahtohallan to learn about Elsa's powers. Elsa is determined to find Ahtohallan—on her own, to keep Olaf and Anna safe. When her sister leaves her behind, Anna is heartbroken.

On her journey, Elsa encounters the Water Nokk, the horse-shaped spirit of water. It carries her to the banks of Ahtohallan, where she follows the mysterious voice into an ice cave.

"I hear you. And I'm coming," says Elsa.

Elsa sees a memory-image of her mother, Iduna, flickering on the cave wall. Iduna helps Elsa understand who she is meant to be—not the Queen of Arendelle, but the Snow Queen, the connection between humans and nature!

More memories appear, and Elsa soon learns the terrible truth: her grandfather caused the battle between Arendelle and the Northuldra—and the curse on the forest.

Elsa goes deeper into Ahtohallan, and finds she has gone too far. She becomes encased in ice! With her last breath, she sends an image out to Anna, revealing the secret to freeing the Enchanted Forest.

Anna and Olaf are trapped in a cave when they receive Elsa's icy message. Then Olaf begins to flurry! Anna knows that means Elsa is gone, too. Even though she is deeply sad, she picks herself up. She finds a way out of the cave. And she knows what she must do: destroy the dam, even though it will also destroy Arendelle.

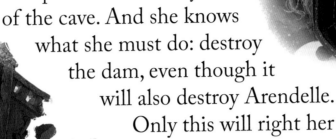

Only this will right her grandfather's wrongs. Anna wakes the Earth Giants, shouting, "Throw your boulders!"

The boulders smash the dam—and Anna's selfless act frees her sister! Elsa races to Arendelle, arriving just in time to save their home.

Arendelle is safe, the curse lifts, and Olaf comes back to life! Anna, now Queen of Arendelle, has learned how strong she is. And Elsa, the Snow Queen, is finally where her powers can do the most good. Together, the sisters have mended the kingdom and the forest.

STRONGER TOGETHER!

In the forest, the friends are introduced to the spirits of nature. The Wind Spirit blows a swirling vortex that has them spinning and twisting. Help the friends find these things that have spun away:

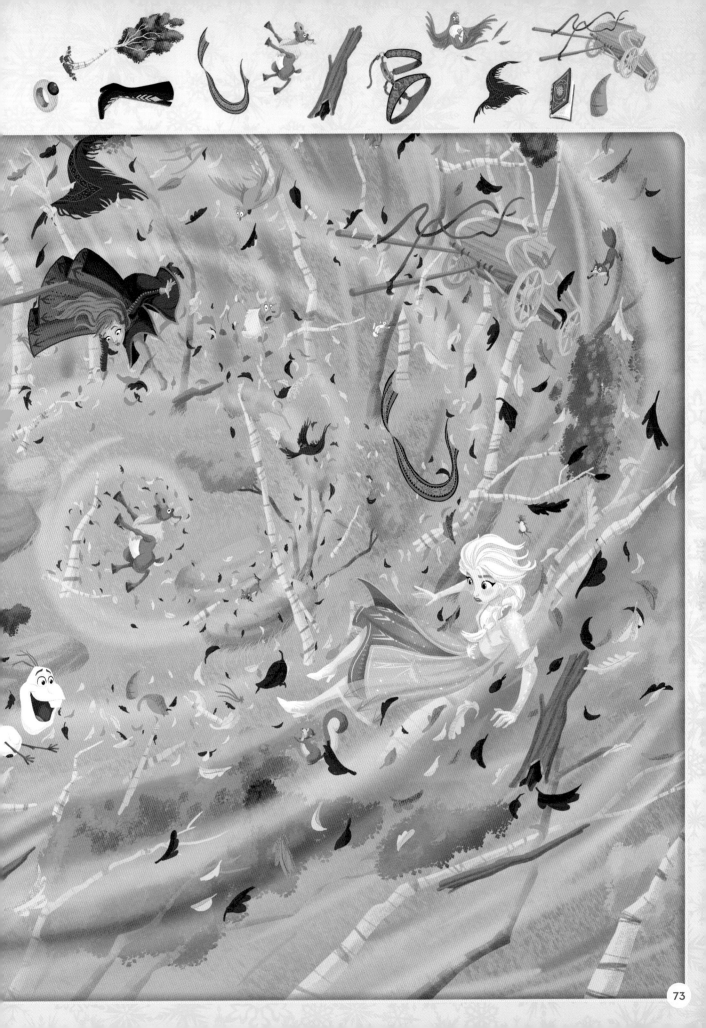

Soon after the friends meet the Northuldra people in the
Enchanted Forest, the Fire Spirit arrives and forges a fiery path!
Can you keep your cool and find these forest friends and items?

As the friends learn about the Northuldra people, Earth Giants come looking for Elsa. While she creates a diversion to send them on their lumbering way, find these things, both earthly and magical:

Alone, Elsa encounters another force of nature: the Water Nokk, a majestic horse that embodies the power of water. Elsa must earn its respect before it will let her reach her destination. Dive in and find these icy blasts and rugged rocks:

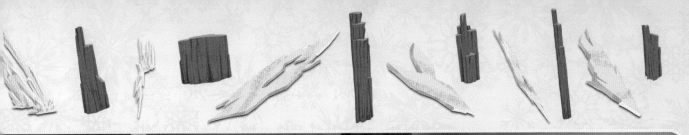

Congratulations!

You made it to the end of the book.
A book is like a warm hug—you can really get
wrapped up in the story.
When you're ready, go back
to the beginning and
take another look...

Some books are worth reading again!